CAT HEADS

Written and Illustrated by

Christine Rasmussen

◆ FriesenPress

Suite 300 - 990 Fort St
Victoria, BC, V8V 3K2
Canada

www.friesenpress.com

ISBN
978-1-5255-8190-8 (Hardcover)
978-1-5255-8191-5 (Paperback)
978-1-5255-8192-2 (eBook)

1. Juvenile Fiction, Animals, Cats

Distributed to the trade by The Ingram Book Company

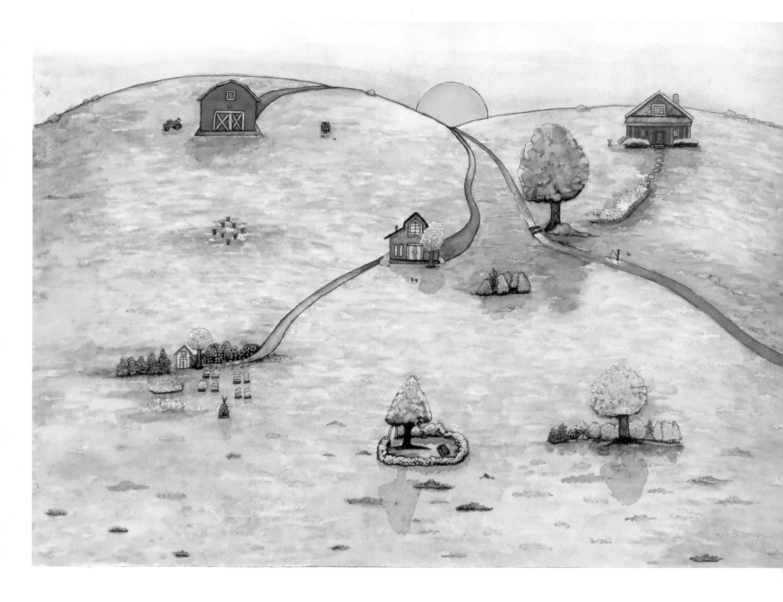

Ramona and Abby,
our favourite pets,

can get into mischief.
Those crazy cat heads!

Abby waits by her dish
'cuz she wants to be fed.

So, she sends up Ramona
to wake us from bed.

Abby likes to sneak outside.
She thinks we won't see her
when she tries to hide.

"Get away from the door!
We still see you, Abby!"
She narrows her eyes and walks away, crabby.

All of a sudden, a fly whizzes by,
catching the attention of our cat heads' eyes.

Ramona
jumped up
onto the
screen door,
and then
Abby's gone!
We see her
no more.

Abby enjoys herself, wandering about...

...Not knowing the neighbour has let his dog out.

The dog thinks it's fun
to chase Abby around,
so she runs to a place where
she hopes she won't be found.

She stays there,
so scared,
eyes scanning
the ground.
But before she
knows it,
the sun goes down.

For two days
and two nights...

... We search throughout the farm.

Inside
and
outside...

... We scour the barn.

We search
every place
that Abby
might roam.

But for two days and nights,
she doesn't come home.

We worry and worry! Then on day three, we hear a soft meowing from up in a tree.

Hooray! Hooray! We've found our Abby!

We climb
up the tree
to bring
Abby home,
Who now
knows it's no
good to sneak
off alone.

Ramona's excited to see her again.
She's happy to have found her very best friend!

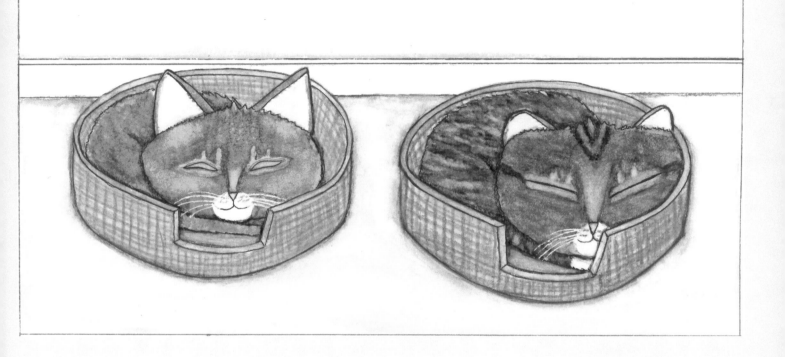

Good night, good night,
you crazy cat heads!

Your adventure is over.
Now off to your beds!

CPSIA information can be obtained
at www.ICGtesting.com
Printed in the USA
BVHW021352030521
606330BV00002B/105